Hattie the Dancing Hippo

Jillian Powell
and Emma Dodson

GROWING MINDS WITH MUSIC

TWIN SISTERS

Send all inquiries to:
Twin Sisters Productions, LLC
4710 Hudson Drive
Stow, OH 44224 USA

ISBN-13 978-159922-726-9

Printed in China.

Hattie wanted to dance.

She tried ballet.

No-one could lift her.

She tried ballroom.

No-one would dance with her.

She tried tap…

...then jive.

"I'll never be a dancer," Hattie thought.

She tried one more class.

She wobbled.

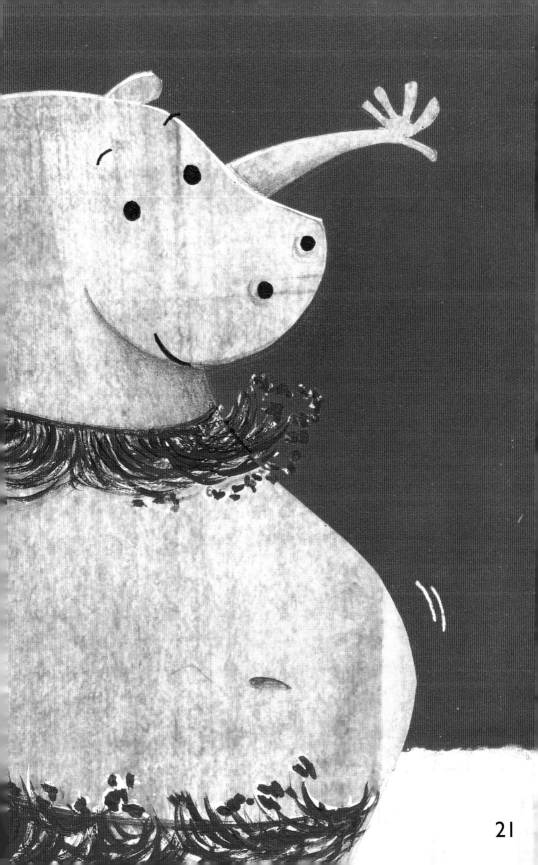

She wiggled.

She waggled.

Hattie was belly-dancing.

She was the best in class!

Reading to your child is the MOST important step in helping your child become a proficient reader. "Hattie The Dancing Hippo" is a humorous story that will engage your child's imagination and encourage the love of reading. Read through the story together. Then, ask your child to point to familiar words. Repetition is the key. Soon your child will be reading and retelling the story to you! Ask the comprehension questions suggested. Reading and comprehension go hand in hand with the "Successful Reader Series." Find a quiet place and enjoy the beauty of reading a book together!

WORDS I KNOW!

to	wanted	dance
she	could	lift
her	with	tap
then	never	more
one	best	

wobbled	**wiggled**	**waggled**
never	**ballet**	**thought**
jive	**tried**	**ballroom**
dancer	**belly-dancing**	

THINK ABOUT IT!

1. What did Hattie want to do?
2. Did Hattie do well at every type of dance she tried?
3. Do you think this story could really happen? Why or why not?

THE STORY AND YOU!

1. What new activity would you like to try?
2. Tell about a time when you tried something new for the first time.
3. Tell about an activity you don't do well.

Draw a picture of you doing your favorite type of dance.